*Bone up on fascinating facts
as you record your own dog days*

with

The
Dog's Digest
Fact-a-day
DIARY

This diary belongs to:

Gromit

Please sign or pawmark here

Free to all subscribers to Dog's Digest,
the fact-packed monthly for the cleverer canine.

Tuesday 13th

The Giant Vegetable Competition is so close, and my marrow's coming along grand. Tucked her up for the night, and had a quick measure — she's grown another 3 mm since last night. Excellent progress! Ran the usual checklist:

. slug damage — CLEAR
. mildew — CLEAR
. blotch — CLEAR
. mosaic virus — CLEAR
. greenhouse humidity — OPTIMUM
. soil moisture — OPTIMUM
. electric blanket — ON (chilly night forecast)
. classical music — ON (*Marrow of Figaro*)
. security systems — ARMED

I've followed every bit of advice in *Maximize Your Marrow*, and it's paid off — she looks stunning. Should be at her very best for Saturday's competition and first prize could be mine! Imagine that — me, the first canine ever to win the Tottington Golden Carrot Award. This dog will have his day!

Trouble is, my marrow's not the only one swelling daily. Wallace's expanding waistline is worrying. I've had him on a cheese-free diet for a while now, but it's not making a blind bit of difference. He still gets stuck in the

Wallace & Gromit
CURSE OF THE
WERE-RABBIT

Dog Diaries

PUFFIN BOOKS

Published by the Penguin Group
Penguin Books Ltd, 80 Strand, London WC2R 0RL, England
Penguin Group (USA) Inc., 375 Hudson Street, New York, New York 10014, USA
Penguin Group (Canada), 90 Eglinton Avenue East, Suite 700, Toronto, Ontario,
Canada M4P 2Y3 (a division of Pearson Penguin Canada Inc.)
Penguin Ireland, 25 St Stephen's Green, Dublin 2, Ireland
(a division of Penguin Books Ltd)
Penguin Group (Australia), 250 Camberwell Road, Camberwell, Victoria 3124,
Australia (a division of Pearson Australia Group Pty Ltd)
Penguin Books India Pvt Ltd, 11 Community Centre, Panchsheel Park, New Delhi –
110 017, India
Penguin Group (NZ), cnr Airborne and Rosedale Roads, Albany, Auckland 1310, New
Zealand (a division of Pearson New Zealand Ltd)
Penguin Books (South Africa) (Pty) Ltd, 24 Sturdee Avenue, Rosebank,
Johannesburg 2196, South Africa

Penguin Books Ltd, Registered Offices: 80 Strand, London WC2R 0RL, England

www.penguin.com

First published 2005
3

Made and printed in England by Clays Ltd, St Ives plc

British Library Cataloguing in Publication Data
A CIP catalogue record for this book is available from the British Library

ISBN 0–141–318880

Dog Diaries

By Richard Dungworth

Screenplay by Mark Burton, Bob Baker,
Steve Box and Nick Park

PUFFIN

My marrow and me.

Get-U-Up exit hatch most mornings.

Maybe it's his age — he's pushing 220 (or whatever that is in human years) but I don't think he's taking the cheese ban seriously. He's just *mad* for the stuff! I found him watching his *Tai Cheese: Exercising with Edam* video yesterday, drooling like a bulldog. It's about time I got tough on him — must sort out an action plan.

Our new jobs should help to get him in tip-top form. We've been so busy since this Anti-pesto idea took off. Protecting people's vegetables is great but answering emergency calls 24/7 (and mainly at night) is wearing me out!

Take last night, for example:

CALL-OUT LOG: 12th/13th SEPTEMBER

23.30 FALSE ALARM
Mr Growbag, returning from pub to wrong house

01.40 VIP (Vegetable-plot Intrusion in Progress)
        INTRUDER AT MRS MULCH'S APPREHENDED

03.10 FALSE ALARM
Mrs Mulch sleepwalking

Haven't had a proper night's sleep since we started the business. So much for letting sleeping dogs lie! But I love it! Wallace and me – the old team on form! We're on High Alert right now, with the competition so close, and everyone's vegetables reaching their prime. We've installed at least forty Garden Gnome Alarms in the last month. There can't be a conservatory in town we haven't fitted with Greenhouse Easi-locks. At this rate we'll be able to retire by Christmas. I've done so much wire-stripping and soldering. Even had to raid our old moon-rocket in the cellar for parts.

The exercise is great for Wallace, and the job's given him real purpose. Before he came up with Anti-pesto, he was spending most of his time inventing contraptions to 'make my life easier' – which none of them did.

Truth is, I was beginning to dread trying out the next gadget. His Dog-Bath-O-Matic nearly drowned me a couple of months ago, and the milkman's not been back since the Slipper-and-Paper-Fetch-Otron short-circuited and chased after him. You'd think Wallace would have learned his lesson after the fiasco with those awful automatic dog-walking trousers . . .

Anti-pesto! We're on high alert.

Anyhow, now Anti-pesto is up and running, there's loads he can busy himself with. He's got the automated launch running smoothly now, and the Rabbit-Grab Mk. III has stopped going off unexpectedly, like the early versions.

We've been working hard on our Apprehend-and-Neutralize manoeuvres, too – including a couple of slick set pieces with some rolling and jumping added in.

Worried what I'm supposed to do with all the rabbits we've nabbed. The cellar's filling up fast, and it's taking me ages to chop the carrots each time they need feeding. I'm hoping

Wallace doesn't come up with one of his solutions to speed this up. I've spotted him pondering the knife rack.

Anyway, I think I'll re-read the marrow section in *Green Paws: A Dog's Gardening Guide* then get some sleep. It's bound to be another busy night!

W's weightloss - things to do

booby-trap 'secret' bookcase cheese stash

cancel magazine subscription to
Wensleydale Weekly

cancel satellite subscription to
Channel Cheese

reserve *Creative Crackers: Cheeseless but not
Tasteless* at library

confiscate cheeseboard/knife and other
cheese-related items

instigate 'no cheese chat' house-rule

Wallace and his cheese-free diet.

Wednesday 14th

Can't sleep. Just tried to relax by doing a spot of knitting. Added a few new rows to the tank top I'm knitting for Wallace (he says his old one's shrunk!) but I'm dropping stitches like nobody's business.

I've got this feeling that something bad has happened, but I'm not sure *what*. I was checking on my marrow this evening (another 2 mm growth, which is excellent) when I had this strange sense - call it canine intuition - that something wasn't right.

Maybe it was this evening's experiment that unsettled me. I just *knew* Wallace would want to figure out some way to tackle our rabbit accommodation problem, especially after we took in a whole new bunch of bunny inmates this morning.

We'd had an unexpected phone call from Lady Tottington of Tottington Hall, just after breakfast. She's not one of our regular clients, but she'd seen the fantastic front-page piece on us in today's paper and thought we'd be able to deal with her 'major infestation' humanely.

When we got up to the Hall in the van - extremely posh place - there were rabbits

One for the scrapbook...

everywhere. It would have taken forever to pick them off individually, so we used the Bun-Vac to hoover them up.

The latest bagless Bun-Vac model is a great machine. It worked really well (plenty of suction) and sucked up every rabbit in the grounds in minutes. Unfortunately, it also sucked up a local posh toff — Victor Something-or-other. He was *very* grumpy about it. Turns out he'd been all set to *shoot* the rabbits, when our machine got hold of him.

He had this growly little canine sidekick with him. The dumb sort that chases parked cars. He had a sniff at me, and gave me the old growl-yap-yap intimidation routine.

Anyway, something Lady Tottington said to Wallace gave him the madcap idea that we really might be able to *brainwash* the rabbits we'd captured. Then they wouldn't *want* to eat everyone's vegetables, and we could set them free again.

Wallace has been developing this new Mind-Manipulation-O-Matic machine anyway. He'd been finding the No Cheese Diet so hard that inventing something to get rid of his cheese cravings seemed the best idea. He was going to try it out on himself this morning to clear his mind of cheesy thoughts — when we were interrupted by a

Need half a dozen more balls of green four-ply. Didn't realize I'd used so much for this tank top...

call from Her Ladyship, thank goodness.

So Wallace spent this afternoon, after we got back from the Hall, connecting the Mind-Manipulation machine to the Bun-Vac. We had to wait until the moon came out this evening to power up the lunar cells using moonshine. Wallace popped on the Mind-O-Matic helmet - so he could generate vegetable-hating mind-waves - and I switched the Bun-Vac lever to 'suck'.

Things would've been fine, and I was actually coming round to the idea that this could really work, when Wallace somehow knocked the lever to 'blow'. One rabbit (the one we caught trying to nab Mrs Mulch's prize pumpkin last night) got blown out of the Bun-Vac cylinder right into the helmet. Wallace started howling like a wolfhound and I had to smash the helmet.

Wallace *seems* fine, though. He hasn't mentioned cheese *once* this evening, which is a huge step forward. He even tucked into the veggie pie I cooked for supper. And the little rabbit - Wallace has called him Hutch - has certainly gone right off his carrots. So it looks like the experiment was a success.

Anyway, better get to bed. Some small fluffy felon is bound to be planning a garden assault even as I write this . . .

Caught in the act!

Friday 16th

The last forty-eight hours have been a whirlwind and it's far from over. No idea where Wallace is and I don't think I've really come to terms with *what* he is, either . . .

It all started yesterday morning. I woke up from my first undisturbed night's sleep for a long while, feeling like a different dog. Did my usual ten minutes of Pooch Pilates, then went downstairs to fix the bunnies their breakfast. I was just assuming that for once there'd been no pest-related incidents in the night.

I couldn't have been more wrong. Downstairs, I found *every one* of our Client Alert Indicators flashing madly. There wasn't a single Gnome Alarm that hadn't been triggered. It was just typical that Wallace's wake-up launch system had chosen that very night to fail. The Trigger Kettle had been nudged off the gas ring, so we'd slept soundly through a night of utter vegetable carnage.

It was all over the *Morning Post* paper. Something had devastated the town's vegetable plots overnight and we'd made the headlines again for all the wrong reasons:

The phone was ringing off the hook with one angry Anti-pesto client after another, wanting to know why we hadn't saved their veg. There was even an emergency meeting at the church and it wasn't pretty. Everyone was hopping mad — we do take our vegetables *very* seriously round here.

Then the vicar arrived, ranting about having come face to face with the culprit the previous night — he says it's an eight-foot-tall giant 'Were-rabbit' come to punish us.

What a difference a day makes . . .

Of course, that snarling little mutt and his murderous master, Victor Whatshisface, turned up right on cue, offering to hunt the big bunny.

Wallace and his 'big idea'

Fortunately, Lady Tottington wouldn't let them shoot it and insisted that Wallace and I have a chance to catch it humanely first. The townsfolk weren't so sure, but Wallace impressed them with his big idea of catching the big rabbit with 'a Big Trap' - his very words. Honestly, I don't know how he gets away with it sometimes! It's a good job they're a simple bunch.

So we rushed home to figure out a way of capturing the giant rabbit. Wallace reckoned we might be able to lure it with a female rabbit decoy. Anyway, by evening, we'd managed to run up a fairly lifelike giant lady rabbit and fix her to the van's roof. Wallace rigged her with strings so I could make her move 'alluringly' from inside the van while he drove. I always get the best jobs!

Looking 'alluring!'

I was just putting our lady rabbit through a great high-kicking, eyelash-fluttering number, when Wallace drove into a low tunnel, and she got knocked off. The strings slammed me hard against the van roof, which really hurt!

While Wallace went back to fetch the bunny, I peeled myself off the roof, detached myself from the strings and sat up front to wait. But Wallace was gone for ages and I started to get the jitters sitting there on my own — especially because we'd stopped right outside a fruit and veg shop. I managed to knit a few more rows of Wallace's tank top, to pass the time and calm my nerves, but it was very quiet and eerie.

Suddenly, out of nowhere, the giant rabbit appeared! I beeped the horn, like, to get Wallace's attention, but he didn't show — I know why *now*. There was nothing else I could do, but set off after the huge bunny myself.

Blimey, he moved fast! I'd only just managed to get the van's Auto Lasso looped around it when it began to burrow furiously, dragging the van and me deep underground.

It burrowed around for ages, kicking up mud and totally covering the van until it tunnelled right under Mrs Girdling's greenhouse. There was a massive crash and the whole greenhouse collapsed into the tunnel, trapping the van and breaking the lasso. Within seconds, the giant rabbit had tunnelled out of sight and I was left stranded, with a muzzle full of airbag.

The van was completely covered with soil. By the time I got it running again, and followed the long tunnel ahead back to the surface, the sun was coming up.

Hutch

Surprised to resurface *in our back garden*. Was really worried that the giant bunny had munched my marrow. She was fine, thank goodness, but the giant muddy bunny prints led straight through our back door . . .

Wallace was fielding more angry calls from clients as I walked in. Loads of people had suffered a second night of vegetable carnage and

I was in the doghouse, of course, for driving off without him.

I was more worried about the bunny tracks and ignored Wallace while I followed the giant prints to the cellar. Wallace followed me down there, and we found Hutch's hutch in shatters, with the little rabbit sleeping off a huge feed! Wallace was as convinced as I was that we'd created and caught the mysterious Were-rabbit.

Wallace set off immediately to tell Lady Tottington that we'd caught the rabbit monster, leaving me to knock up a giant rabbit-proof enclosure for Hutch. Managed to create a

monstrous cage in minutes, although I could've done with a bit of help from Wallace. I'm not just a dogsbody.

Wasn't till I'd finished reinforcing the cellar door that I noticed that the giant rabbit prints actually led *past* the cellar, not into it. I followed them up the stairs and got such a shock! The rabbit prints changed into human footprints and they led straight into Wallace's room!

I couldn't believe it at first, but it fitted perfectly. *That's* why he hadn't turned up when the giant rabbit showed up last night. Wallace *was* the giant rabbit! The experiment really had gone very wrong! And if the moon triggered his transformation, I had to get Wallace back from Tottington Hall before nightfall.

So, I shot over to Tottington Hall, scaled the wall and spotted Wallace with Her Ladyship up in the rooftop conservatory. Wallace was surrounded by temptation – magnificent veg of every variety. I knew I had to get him out of there, and *fast*, but I couldn't see how.

Then I spotted the sprinkler system trigger and managed to hit it with a well-aimed asparagus spear. The downpour soon caught his attention!

Wallace was fairly put out with me on the drive home but he had no idea how much trouble he could've been in. All I cared about was getting him back to West Wallaby Street before nightfall.

I was going flat out, following a diversion through Clopplethorpe Wood when suddenly I had to pull up short to avoid hitting a tree lying

Enemy Number One

across the road. Wallace got out to take a look, and that horrible Victor man and his short-legged sidekick sprang out of nowhere - it was an ambush!

Apparently, Victor didn't appreciate Wallace's friendliness towards Lady Tottington and was all set to rough him around a bit. I tried to get out to help, but that thug of a mutt kept me penned in the van.

They got more than they bargained for, though. Just as Victor was flexing his muscles, the moon came out and Wallace started to tremble. Before our eyes, in a matter of moments, my old friend turned from man to rabbit monster - an eight-foot furry buck-toothed fiend! He threw the fallen tree aside, and bounded off into the wood. I set off after him in the van, leaving those two hunting half-wits boggle-eyed behind me.

I couldn't keep up with him, though - never seen anything move so fast. I gave up after a while and came back home, hoping he might be here, but no luck.

He's out there somewhere, causing veg havoc and the Client Alert Indicators are going crazy again. What has Wallace done to himself?! What am I going to do? My head's spinning like I've been chasing my tail . . .

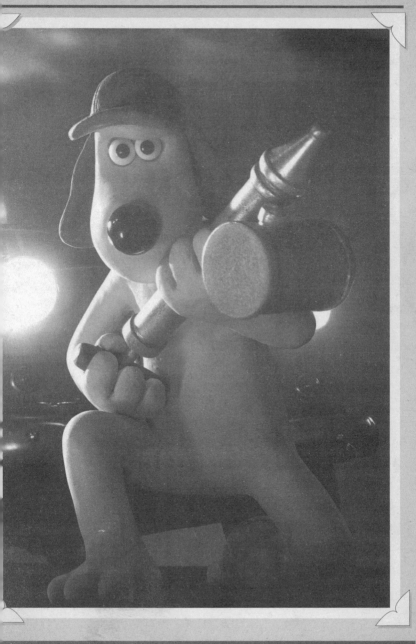

spire the invention of dominoes

Saturday 17th

The night of the Giant Vegetable Competition!

Woof — what a day! But hurrah — Wallace is back (and sleeping off the effects of several tail-tingling hours spent dodging bullets) and I've won the Tottington Golden Carrot Award! Can't quite believe it. But my beloved marrow's bed is empty, which is tragic but there was no other way . . .

Woke early, hoping that yesterday's events had

all been a bad dream but the morning paper confirmed the worst. My heart sank as I scanned the reports of the overnight vegetable chaos caused by 'the Beast'.

I had no choice but to tell Wallace what he'd become. I pulled the Get-U-Up lever warily because I really wasn't sure what to expect. Wallace landed at the breakfast table in the middle of a stream of half-eaten vegetables. I was relieved to see he'd made it home, and returned to human form – almost – but he still had a pair of long, furry ears!

Love my ears!

I'm rather fond of my own long ears – they're
quite distinguished – but a rabbit-eared Wallace
is a different matter and they looked very odd.
I showed them to him in the hand-mirror, and
pointed to the front-page headlines, hoping he'd
twig what I meant.

He wasn't having any of it – dismissed his new

ears as a side-effect of his vegetable diet. Called me a 'silly old pooch' for thinking they meant anything more!

Something he said got me thinking that if *he* had become part-rabbit during the Mind-Manipulation fiasco, maybe *Hutch's* strange behaviour was down to the fact that *he* had become

selves be tied to railings in protest

part-*Wallace*. Perhaps each of them had somehow taken on a little of the other's nature.

Sure enough, when I checked on Hutch, his transformation into a slippered and tank-topped cheese-lover was clear to see – clear enough, in fact, to make even Wallace take on board the rabbity reality of his own situation. What a mess!

Understandably, Wallace needed a little time to come to terms with the proper pickle he'd got us into. I brewed him a nice cup of tea – always helps in a crisis. Then we set about trying to get him back to his old all-human self by fixing the Mind-Manipulation-O-Matic, in the hope that we could reverse the brainwashing experiment.

But the part of Wallace's mind used for all things contraption-related is the part that's been 'manipulated'. He's just too preoccupied with carrots and lettuce to tell his diodes from his transistors.

Couldn't find anything helpful in *Electronics for Dogs* either, and Hutch just kept wittering on about cheese and knitwear. He can be irritating to have around, but it's not his fault, I suppose. By this evening, we'd got nowhere and Wallace was getting desperate.

To make matters worse, Lady Tottington called round and I only just managed to grab Hutch before he answered the door and gave the game away. Wallace hid his ears under a hat, and tried to talk to Lady Tottington on the doorstep without raising her suspicions, but dusk was falling and I could tell Wallace couldn't concentrate.

I overheard Lady Tottington say that after last night's vegetable casualties, she had finally agreed to let that Victor *hunt down and shoot the Were-rabbit*! That gave me the goosebumps, especially when I could see Wallace's bunny ears poking out of his hat!

As the moon emerged, Wallace started to change again. He only just managed to get rid of Her Ladyship before he sprouted huge furry hands, enormous feet and in minutes became a fully transformed eight-foot, vegetable-obsessed, giant bunny.

So when I spotted that muscle-bound hunting mutt and his master outside, I knew I didn't have a minute to lose.

I grabbed our lady rabbit suit and climbed inside, hoping I'd look enough like a large alluring lady rabbit to tempt rabbit-brained Wallace out into our back garden. In desperation, I set off across the neighbouring gardens on my space-hopper, with giant rabbit-Wallace still tagging along.

Then there was a gunshot! I was bowled muzzle-over-tail by Victor's first shot — he was even using gold bullets! Next thing I knew, I was being dragged out of the lady rabbit suit and shoved inside one of our Anti-pesto traps by Victor, while his dense dog chuckled smugly. I was glad they'd got hold of *me*, rather than Wallace, who'd hopped off hungrily, but once they were sure I was locked up nice and tight, Victor and that mutt set off after him anyway.

I spent a few minutes trying to lever the trap open with an old garden trowel, but it soon snapped. Our traps are titanium-reinforced — you get top quality when you enrol with Anti-pesto, you know. Unluckily for me!

Then I spotted a nearby Gnome Alarm. I could hear Hutch up in Wallace's bedroom, and I hit on the best idea! I threw the trowel handle at the alarm as hard as I could and managed to set the alarm off (and fling Hutch into the launch mode). Seconds later, our van burst through the back wall of our garage, with Hutch at the wheel. It crashed into the trap I was in and freed me!

My mind was racing. I was sure the Were-rabbit would head for the vegetable competition and

People at the Giant Vegetable Competition looking worried

Victor would work this out, too. I had to come up with something to tempt the hungry bunny away from the competition stands or Wallace was going to hop right into Victor's gun-sights.

Then it came to me. My marrow – the ultimate vegetable temptation. It broke my heart to sacrifice it, but I couldn't see any other way to save Wallace from certain death. I rushed to the greenhouse, cut my marrow's stalk with a trembling paw and gave her to Hutch to hold in the van.

I drove like a mad dog to Tottington Hall. When

we reached the grounds of the Hall, I roped my marrow up behind the van, sat astride her as Hutch took the wheel, and off we set to catch ourselves a Wallace Were-rabbit.

We weren't a moment too soon. By the time we roared on to the scene, the giant rabbit was heading for the main competition stand, with Victor standing in front of the crowd taking his final aim.

My magnificent marrow did the trick! Wallace the Were-rabbit couldn't resist it - as I shot past, he changed direction and followed us eagerly. So things were going to plan - until Hutch lost control and sent us careering into the Cheese Tent and my beloved marrow met her mushy end.

There was no time to mourn. Dazed and confused, I scrambled out of the tent, just in time to see the Were-rabbit climbing up the outside of the Hall tower, with Lady Tottington in his furry grasp, and Victor close behind . . . and then I was set upon by that mutt! (He may be short, but he's very vicious!)

By the time I shook him off, Wallace was on the rooftop, with Victor still in hot pursuit. I knew I had to get up there to help him, but how?

Then I spotted the *Reach For the Skies* fair-
ride nearby. One of its aeroplanes was exactly
what I needed — I've read all the *Red Setter:
Canine Air Cadet* stories, and I reckoned I could
handle a single-seater fighter, no problem.

I soon had the engine humming nicely, but that
annoyingly growly dog was back on my tail, in a
plane of his own. I sped round the helter-skelter
ride as fast as I could to get some speed up and
took off in style, but that dumb dog followed
suit and we were soon locked in a dramatic
dogfight.

Even when his plane spiralled out of control,
it wasn't over — he somehow managed to board *my*
plane and start another fight, till I sent him
plummeting through my bomb doors.

But with all the distractions, it looked like I was going to be too late to save Wallace. I steered my plane over to where Victor had cornered Wallace just as there was a massive BANG! and an enormous golden bullet – the Golden Carrot Award – hurtled towards Wallace. Desperately, I swung my plane around into its path, and just made it!

My plane took the bullet's full force. I thought I'd had it. But as I fell, Wallace bravely leaped from the roof and clutched me in his giant furry rabbit paws. We tore through the roof of the Cheese Tent below and hit the ground with a right old thump.

And the danger *still* hadn't passed. Outside the Cheese Tent, I could hear the crowd getting angrier and angrier. They were coming closer to the tent, determined to finish off the Beast.

I didn't have a clue what to do, until an answer fell from the skies – Victor, smacked off the roof by Lady Tottington and her giant carrot, tumbled through the tent, landed on the roof of our nearby van, forced its doors to swing open and revealed the lady rabbit suit. A plan came to me in a flash. While Victor was still dazed, I shoved him inside the suit, and pushed him,

tottering around in confusion, out of the tent.

It worked! I heard the mob give a bloodthirsty shout, and, thinking Victor was the Were-rabbit, they hounded him off the Hall grounds. That stupid dog of his even led the pack as they chased him into the woods! At last I could take care of the real Were-rabbit. But my heart sank.

Wallace was lying motionless on the ground. Slowly, he changed back into his old self, but I couldn't get him to wake up. It was awful. After everything we'd been through, I thought I'd lost my faithful friend. Lady Tottington tried to comfort me. She knew Wallace's secret now, too, but I was inconsolable.

As the tears rolled down my nose, it picked up the faintest whiff of hope – a cheesy whiff. Of course! If anything could revive Wallace, it had to be *cheese*. I grabbed a plate of Stinging Bishop cheese from Hutch, who was gorging himself nearby, and wafted a piece under Wallace's nose.

I held my breath. Minutes past, but eventually Wallace's nose began to twitch. He stirred, revived by the cheesy smell, and came round at last!

Other than feeling a bit bruised, and embarrassed about finding himself naked in front of Lady Tottington (I've never understood what it is about humans and clothes), Wallace was fine.

So *that* is how I nearly lost my oldest friend.

What a mad day! We'll have to come up with a solution to Wallace's rabbit problem at some point, but at least for tonight, he's safe.

And as for my marrow – well, her end was tragic and mushy but it was also glorious! Just after Wallace came round, Lady Tottington presented me with the Golden Carrot Award – for 'a brave and splendid marrow,' she said.

I'm so proud. Got the award with me now, on my bedside table. It's a bit battered from being used as ammunition by that Victor thug, but I don't care. First thing tomorrow, I'll give it a good polish . . .

ake themselves dry

Monday 26th

Things are more or less back to normal, at last. Well, as normal as we're used to!

We've just got back from releasing the rabbits. Yep — we let them go! Not into the community, of course. Lady Tottington has set up a high-security Rabbit Sanctuary in the grounds of Tottington Hall. Any rabbits we catch in the future will be able to live there happily — without putting the town's vegetables at risk.

Hutch went to the Sanctuary too. He and Wallace are back to their old selves now, thank goodness. We eventually managed to repair the Mind-O-Matic, and reverse the brainwashing. There's no point in wishing Wallace would stop inventing — just next time I hope it doesn't involve brainwashing anything!

Without the rabbits to take care of, I'm going to concentrate on my gardening again and win next year's competition. I'm determined to keep the Golden Carrot Award — it looks great on our mantelpiece, next to Wallace's Alternative Toasting Technologies Runner-Up rosette.

Think I might try something a bit more challenging this time — quite fancy having a shot at the Exotic Fruits, Best In category. I'd

best draw up an action plan — never too soon to start planning when it comes to raising prize produce.

Things to do:

- order seeds

- source quality compost/manure

- get *Pawpaws for Four Paws* from library

- check back issues of *Horticulture For Hounds* for tropical fruit tips

- knit smaller anti-frost blankets

- talk to Wallace about creating tropical micro-climate in understairs cupboard

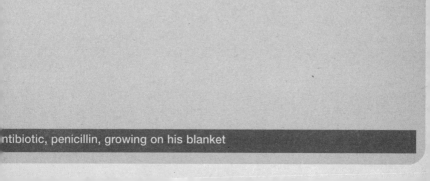
ntibiotic, penicillin, growing on his blanket

SUNDAY

Master's still not home. Dunno where he's got to.

I'm *starving*. Just tried to get the lid off one of my Meaty Chunks tins with my teeth. Crushed the stupid thing.

Drooled so much just thinking about lunch that my blanket's all soggy.

Wonder when he'll be back. Something's not right — I can feel it in my bones. Bones — now there's an idea! Now then, where did I bury that last lot . . . ?

the nearest tent steps the giant rabbit. Well, I'd got that hot under the collar trying to get my teeth into that drippy dog, I was feeling fit to tackle anything, no matter how big.

So I went for him, full on. Got my teeth into his fluffy backside good and proper. He couldn't get out of there fast enough. I chased him well past Clopplethorpe Wood. A fair few of the villagers tagged along, waving pitchforks and what have you.

Don't think he'll be showing his whiskery face round here again in a hurry.

So I was rather hoping I might get a Doggy Treat, or something, from Master.

But there's no sign of him. Never mind. Best get some shut-eye. Guess he'll be back when I wake up . . .

Reckoned it was high time I took that interfering hound out of the picture. But I couldn't lay my paws on him. Somehow he managed to get a plane from a fairground ride up in the air. I jumped in another one, and set off after him.

It was some dogfight, I can tell you. I was hot on his tail the whole while. The number of times I nearly got him ... Even managed to get into his plane!

But then I came a cropper, somehow. Found myself free-falling, fast. Hit the bouncy castle, thank goodness.

Just about got back on my paws, when out of

The villagers were all there. Vegetables everywhere. You should have seen the state they got in when they found out the big bunny was still on the loose. I've not seen chaos like that since Accringley Dog Show, when that Siamese wandered in during the obedience Trials.

Anyhow, all of a sudden, I got a double-nostril-full of weird rabbit-human scent. It was the monster bunny.

Master was sighting up his shot, when that Gromit messed things up again. Turned up riding a marrow of all things, tempting the big bunny out of the line of fire.

a collar? Bet he's one of those sorts of dogs –
thinks he's so much better than the rest of us:
won't wear a collar 'because it represents
enslavement' and won't fetch a stick 'because
it's demeaning'.

Makes me sick. It's what my dad called 'fancy
modern ideas'. I love my collar. Specially the shiny
studs. Makes me look hard.

Anyway, bet old lanky-legs didn't feel so clever
when we shoved him in one of his own pesto cages.

Then we were off after the real rabbit again.
Up to the Hall, where
the big
vegetable show
they'd all been
banging on about
was just kicking
off.

Tottington gave
Master the green
light to hunt down the
giant rabbit.

Master didn't need
asking twice. We were off
to pay a house call on old Wally — aka Big Bunny —
pronto.

Sure enough, found him in furry form. In fact,
there were *two* giant rabbits. Making a break
for it across the back gardens. Master downed
one of them, first shot. But it turned out to be
that annoying dog again — Gromit, I think he's
called — and the shot just got his costume. Which
was some sort of giant lady rabbit get-up.
Unbelievable.

Talk about giving a dog a bad name — he makes
us all look bad. Do you know he doesn't even wear

his master's half-man, half-giant-rabbit monster. I can't operate machinery or drive a van, but I can handle myself. Let's see how much use his oh-so-sharp mind is against a real dog's sharp teeth . . .

Heh-heh-heh! So much for Mr Monster Bunny. Soon had him running scared. Must have chased him for miles. Bet he's hopping into the next county by now.

Just got home. It was a fair old haul back. I'm about ready for my basket.

Don't know where Master's got to. Thought I might be up for a 'well done' pat on the head, or a scratch behind the ear, but there's no sign of him

No surprise that I'm whacked — been on the go non-stop since this afternoon, when Lady

Dunno about going after the Big Bunny now. Might be more trouble than it's worth. Looked pretty chewy, to be honest. 'The thing to remember, Trevor my lad,' my dad used to say (he got my name wrong a lot — I was one of nine), 'is to take care where you cock your leg.' Meaning pick your fights carefully. I think.

I've got a bone to pick with that Pesto pooch, though that's for sure. Soon show him who's Top Dog around here — whether or not

The Wally-Rabbit Thing let out this bloodcurdling howl — makes my fur stand on end just remembering it. Then it thumped the ground with its massive feet, so hard that it made my teeth rattle. Next thing, it had picked up the tree like a twig, thrown it aside, and hopped off into the woods.

My natural survival instincts had kicked in — I was hiding under their van. At least, I was, until that droopy-eared dog roared off after the giant rabbit.

Quickly pulled myself together and followed Master home. He was muttering to himself most of the way. Seemed a lot happier after we'd called in at the vicarage, for some reason.

We even got caught in a thunderstorm on the way back — just to cap off a rotten evening. Go soaked.

was on him like a Rottweiler. I concentrated on his four-legged friend. Bit of quality snarling soon put him off getting out of the van.

Master made it very clear to Wally that he was to stay away from Lady Tottington. Looked like he was about to rough him around a bit, when the weird stuff started to happen.

I picked up a strong rabbity whiff — coming from Wally. He was shaking all over. Then suddenly he started to change. Sprouted fur everywhere, and his teeth and ears got longer and longer. Before you could say 'Jack Russell', he'd transformed completely — into a colossal rabbit!

Hadn't got a clue what he was up to, but I didn't really care — I love it in the woods. There's so much to smell, so many trees to pee up and lots of small furry animals to terrify. You have to keep your wits about you, though. My cousin Keith once tried to put the wind up a 'big squirrel' in a pine tree when he was on holiday. Turned out to be a bear. He still has a bad limp. Talk about barking up the wrong tree.

Anyhow, it was starting to get dark, when old Droopy-Ears and his human friend came along the road in their van (that excuse-for-a-dog was driving — smart aleck).

That's when the penny dropped — Master had set up an ambush!

Sure enough, the bloke — Wally, I think he's called — got out to look at the tree across the road, and Master

Up in her rooftop conservatory thingy. Master was steaming. The last time I saw him that angry was when I left my squeaky ball on the stairs. (He slipped, fell and ended up with his face in my bowl of Meaty Chunks. Looked like a dog's dinner.)

We both stomped on the flowers Master had picked (dunno why I did — just thought I should follow his lead). Next thing, I was tagging along as he headed back home — to pick up an axe — and off we marched to Clopplethorpe Wood to chop down a tree so that it fell across the road.

FRIDAY

I am so glad to see my old basket. What a day!
Just knew there was something funny about
this giant rabbit business. It didn't smell right
at the church. Your nose knows — that's what
Dad would have said.

Started out ok. Master seemed quite cheery
when I took him his paper and slippers first thing.
(Rotten job. Newsprint tastes grim, and when
you've got a super-sensitive nose, Master's
slippers — phew! But it's what you do, isn't it?
Man's Best Friend and all that.)

After lunch — bowl of tasty Rabbit-and-Game-
flavour Bite-size Bones for me — we were off up
to the Hall again. Master must have fancied
another sniff round Her Ladyship.

He was picking her some flowers — hate the
things, make me sneeze — when we heard that
Pesto bloke giggling away with Lady Tottington

THINGS To Do

slippers – take to Master
(add bite marks first)

newspaper – chase delivery
boy, take to Master
(the paper, not the boy)

claws – sharpen on sofa

breath – check still foul

bones – find (in rosebed?)

says the hunt's off for now.

Never mind. That drippy pair couldn't catch a cold, let alone an eight-foot rabbit. Reckon they'll soon be begging Master to take a shot at it.

So, thought I'd get in the mood, and get my nose honed in. Had a bit of a sniff round the giant rabbit's tracks in the churchyard, like you do. (No droppings to work with — perhaps just as well, given its size.) Its scent was a bit, well, odd — rabbity, yeh, but with a hint of something else that I couldn't quite put my paw on.

Nothing me and Master can't cope with. As Master says, 'The bigger they are, the harder they are to miss.' Might do a few extra grab-and-drag exercises before I call it a day, though. Reckon an eight-foot rabbit will take a fair bit of retrieving . . .

same crazy look in my Uncle Rover's
eyes, and he was barking mad.

Anyway, Master soon put them straight. Told
them that all they had to do was to hunt the
thing down and shoot it. And he offered our
services.

But would you believe it — they decided to give
that pansy pooch and his idiot master a chance to
catch the big buck-toothed bruiser instead!
'Humanely', whatever that means. So Master

Vegetable gardens — now there's a weird human thing. Think how many tasty bones you could bury in all that soil if it weren't planted up with rotten, tasteless cabbages. I mean, digging — uh-huh, I get it, you can't beat a good dig. But growing stuff? Nope, can't see the appeal.

Anyhow, everyone's panicked that their vegetables won't make it through the week with this hungry bunny about. There's some sort of big show coming up. Apparently, they've been paying that lanky dog and his mangy master to protect their veg. They were having a good yap at them for letting them down. Heh-heh-heh.

The vicar was ranting about how he'd come face to furry face with this monster rabbit in church last night. Judging by the hole it made when it left through the window, it's one BIG bunny. Made an impression on the vicar all right — looks like he's lost the plot to me. I remember seeing the

THURSDAY

BOW-WOW! There's a giant rabbit on the loose!

I would So like a piece of *his* fluffy behind . . .

Imagine — if I could take down a super-sized bunny. Eight-foot tall, they reckon. *That'd* stop that smug Labrador at the post office yapping on about nailing the Strokleshaw Stag. 'Antlers the size of a moose,' blah, blah, blah. I'd give my hind leg to put him in his place.

Found out about the massive rabbit at church this morning. Master had to go to some sort of village meeting, so I tagged along.

Apparently, the rabbit went on the rampage last night. Raided everyone's gardens. Scoffed the vegetables they've all been fussing over lately.

This time I got yelled at for not attacking it.

Feeling too stirred up to sleep. Need to work off some of this energy. Master's watching A Question of Blood Sport. Think I'll go out and see if I can terrify a cat. Might even put in a session with my knotted-rope toy.

Just hope tomorrow I can get my chops round something more tasty . . .

wasn't sure, not without Master there. But when they pulled Master back out of the ground, he had a good growl at them, anyway.

Somehow, their nasty contraption had collected up all the rabbits in a big glass thing. There wasn't a single one left for us to hunt. So we stomped back home again. Master was in a rotten mood for the rest of the day. Turned out he'd come back wearing a rabbit on his head, instead of his fur-piece thing.

Master's fur-piece missing in action

attacked it — like you would. He gave me a right old boot up the backside.

Anyhow, when Master put his hand down the hole to get his fur back, something pulled him in. Started to drag him along underground, so I followed the lump. Barking, of course — 'If in doubt, son, bark,' that's what my old dad taught me.

Some idiot had stuck a pole right where I was bound to run into it. Fair clouted me, it did. Anyhow, the lump that was Master kept moving till he was sucked out of the ground by a big mechanical-smelling machine.

There was a twerpy-looking human beside it and a dog — long-legged, long-eared — pressing buttons and pulling levers to make it work. Bold as brass. Wearing a hat! Very la-di-dah.

Obviously I growled at them both. Ears back, gums showing, nose wrinkled — I've been working o my snarl lately. Thought about attacking, but

Master took a pop at one of the little vermin nearby — but it dodged the bullet. Amazing, it was. Never seen a rabbit move so fast. It went down its burrow like greased lightening.

When Master took a closer look, his fake fur — the bit he covers the shiny part of his head with shot into the hole, too. Just like the rabbit had.

Master's wig thing is more trouble than it's worth, if you ask me. I dunno what it's for. Maybe if you're human, not having head fur is a bit like losing your tail, or having a dry nose. First time Master wore his wig, I thought it was a rat, and

HAD A RUBBISH DAY.

Didn't get my teeth into a single rabbit. Not one measly little fur-ball.

Started out ok. Trooped off to Tottington Hall with Master, with a nice cool shotgun barrel between my teeth. I love gun-carrying. Just have to remember not to bark. Last time I dropped a gun, it went off. Nearly shot Master in the foot.

It looked very promising up at the Hall. Rabbits everywhere. Lady Tottington didn't seem too chuffed about us planning to shoot them, though — dunno why. (She's got a smashing set of teeth, for a human. Hair like a poodle, though.)

I passed Master his gun — right on cue, like a pro — and got my jaws and legs limbered up, all set to fetch.

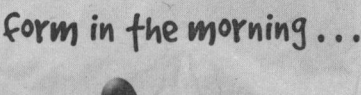

tomorrow's
menu

I'd better rack up a few extra foreleg crunches before basket-time. Need to be on top fetching form in the morning . . .

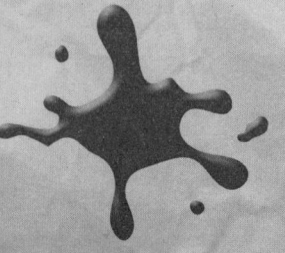

Some of it's my pedigree. I've got Dad's killer nose and camouflage combat markings. But it takes a tough daily workout to get muscle-tone and a jawline like mine.

Should see lots more action tomorrow. We're off up to Tottington Hall. Turns out the grounds are overrun with rabbits. Master's going to shoot as many as possible. Think he's trying to impress Lady Tottington. He's been sniffing round her for a while, seems to think she's got the right breeding for a Quartermaine wife.

It's not for your weedy breeds. Peak physical condition, that's me. Best teeth in the county. Take a look at these...
RRRRRRRRRRRRRRRR!
Pretty impressive, huh?

PHILIP'S SCHEDULE,
TAIL-CHASING,
CHEWY BALL WORK,
WOOFING,
GRAB AND DRAG,
CAT CHASING
the key to my
fighter's physique!

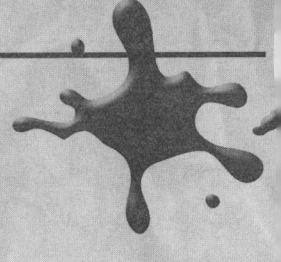

Just put the wind up the
paperboy, good 'n' proper!

Crouched under the hedge until he'd
come through the gate. Then I went for him,
barking and snapping full on. You should have seen
him run!

I'd have had him, too, if I weren't so dog-tired.
Been out hunting all day with Master. I've been so
busy pheasant-fetching, I'm all in. Fantastic fun.
He's a crack shot, my Master. If it moves
BLAM!, he's plugged it. Runs in the Quartermaine
family. Dad used to fetch for Ponsenby
Quartermaine, Master's old man. I remember him
coming home, panting like he was fit to drop. Use
to bag thirty birds in a three-hour shoot. Per
hour, that's . . . um . . . er . . . well, a lot.

Yup, you have to keep in top shape if you're
fetching and gun-carrying for a Quartermaine.

This diary belongs to

Philip

so keep your paws off
or I'll maul ya

Dog Diaries

By Richard Dungworth

Screenplay by Mark Burton, Bob Baker,
Steve Box and Nick Park

PUFFIN

PUFFIN BOOKS

Published by the Penguin Group
Penguin Books Ltd, 80 Strand, London WC2R 0RL, England
Penguin Group (USA) Inc., 375 Hudson Street, New York, New York 10014, USA
Penguin Group (Canada), 90 Eglinton Avenue East, Suite 700, Toronto, Ontario,
Canada M4P 2Y3 (a division of Pearson Penguin Canada Inc.)
Penguin Ireland, 25 St Stephen's Green, Dublin 2, Ireland
(a division of Penguin Books Ltd)
Penguin Group (Australia), 250 Camberwell Road, Camberwell, Victoria 3124,
Australia (a division of Pearson Australia Group Pty Ltd)
Penguin Books India Pvt Ltd, 11 Community Centre, Panchsheel Park, New Delhi –
110 017, India
Penguin Group (NZ), cnr Airborne and Rosedale Roads, Albany, Auckland 1310, New
Zealand (a division of Pearson New Zealand Ltd)
Penguin Books (South Africa) (Pty) Ltd, 24 Sturdee Avenue, Rosebank,
Johannesburg 2196, South Africa

Penguin Books Ltd, Registered Offices: 80 Strand, London WC2R 0RL, England

www.penguin.com

First published 2005
1

© and TM Aardman Animations Ltd 2005. All Rights Reserved. Wallace and Gromit
(word mark) and the characters 'Wallace' and 'Gromit' © and TM
Aardman/Wallace and Gromit Limited.

The moral right of the author and illustrator has been asserted

Made and printed in England by Clays Ltd, St Ives plc

Except in the United States of America, this book is sold subject to the condition that
it shall not, by way of trade or otherwise, be lent, re-sold, hired out, or otherwise
circulated without the publisher's prior consent in any form of binding or cover other
than that in which it is published and without a similar condition including this
condition being imposed on the subsequent purchaser

British Library Cataloguing in Publication Data
A CIP catalogue record for this book is available from the British Library

ISBN 0–141–318880

Dog Diaries